FOR MUM and DAD
WHO FILLED MY LIFE WITH BOOKS

AND FOR OSCAR
WHO PREFERS LOOKING AT THE PICTURES

Q Quarto Knows

Brimming with creative inspiration, how-to projects, and useful
information to enrich your everyday life, Quarto Knows is a favourite
destination for those pursuing their interests and passions. Visit our
site and dig deeper with our books into your area of interest:
Quarto Creates, Quarto Cooks, Quarto Homes, Quarto Lives,
Quarto Drives, Quarto Explores, Quarto Gifts, or Quarto Kids.

Inspiring | Educating | Creating | Entertaining

Text and illustrations © 2018 Grace Easton.
First published in 2018 by Lincoln Children's Books,
an imprint of The Quarto Group.
The Old Brewery, 6 Blundell Street, London N7 9BH, United Kingdom.
T (0)20 7700 6700 F (0)20 7700 8066 www.QuartoKnows.com

A catalogue record for this book is available from the British Library.
ISBN 978-1-78603-031-3
The illustrations were created digitally.
Handlettered and set in Futura
Published by Katie Cotton
Commissioned by Jenny Broom
Designed by Zoë Tucker
Edited by Kate Davies
Production by Jenny Cundill and Kate O'Riordan
Manufactured in Guangdong, China CC122017

1 3 5 7 9 8 6 4 2

GRACE EASTON

CANNONBALL CORALIE AND THE LION

Lincoln Children's
First Editions

There was a little girl who lived in the woods, who didn't like rules. Her name was Coralie.

She could swing from tree to tree,

ROAR!

and juggle five squirrels at a time,

and stand on her hands.

She was funny and brave
and silly and strange.

But no one was there to see her.

Until one day, marching through the woods came acrobats and trumpeters, drummers and jugglers, and best of all...

A LION!

They seemed loud and brave and exciting and odd –
a lot like Coralie. Coralie decided to follow them.

They arrived at a place Coralie had never seen
before, full of lights and colours and daring tricks.
And there, in the middle of it all, was the lion.

Coralie thought he was wonderful.

'ROAR!'

said Lion, which meant,
'Would you like to play with me?
We could do tricks together.
If we're allowed...'

And Coralie said, 'Yes, please.'

She found a man in a big hat, who was telling everyone what to do.

'LESS WOBBLING!'

'MORE BANANAS!'

'AND ABSOLUTELY NO JAZZ!'

he shouted.

He looked in charge, so Coralie asked, 'Please can I stay here with you all? I may be small but I can do all sorts of tricks. And I would like to be friends with your lion.'

The Man in the Big Hat looked at her and said,

'WE DON'T HAVE FRIENDS HERE, BUT LET ME SEE WHAT YOU CAN DO.'

Coralie could balance
very high,

and juggle
cats and dogs,

and pull rabbits out of hats.

'ROAR!' said Lion, which meant, 'You are very talented, for a human so small!'

But the Man in the Big Hat was not impressed. 'Your tricks are not good enough,' he said. 'But you are just the right size to be...'

'...A HUMAN CANNONBALL!'

Being a human cannonball is harder than it looks. You need:

PROTECTIVE GOGGLES

SAFETY HELMET

RED FLYING CAPE

BIG SMILE

POINTY FINGERS

A special outfit,

SUPER-STRONG MUSCLES

an impressive flying pose,

PIZZAZZ

NOT SCARED OF HEIGHTS

FEARLESSNESS

and most importantly, to be extremely brave.

Coralie was extremely brave.
But the cannon was extremely tall.
'What if I can't do it?' said Coralie.

'ROAR!'
said Lion, which meant,
'I think you can do anything!'

That night, Coralie stroked Lion for luck.
As she climbed into the cannon, the jugglers
and acrobats and trumpeters all held their breath.

Coralie shut her eyes tight,
held her chin to the sky and then...

The crowd hollered and clapped and whooped and cheered! Coralie felt as though she might explode with happiness.

ROAR!

said Lion, which meant, 'You were amazing!'

But the Man in the Big Hat didn't look happy at all.

'YOUR ARMS WEREN'T STRAIGHT, YOU DIDN'T POINT YOUR TOES, YOUR LANDING WAS FLOPPY AND YOU DIDN'T DO A SINGLE SOMERSAULT.

PACK YOUR BAGS AND

GO!'

Coralie didn't have any bags to pack, but she did have someone to say goodbye to. 'I'll miss you,' she said to Lion, and she hugged him very tight.

Lion started to follow Coralie – but then the
Man in the Big Hat appeared, and shouted:

'GET BACK TO WORK!
MORE TRICKS!
LESS SMILING!
AND ABSOLUTELY
NO CARING ABOUT
EACH OTHER!'

Lion looked at the Man in the Big Hat
– and so much anger and sadness swelled up
inside him that he let out a loud, lonely...

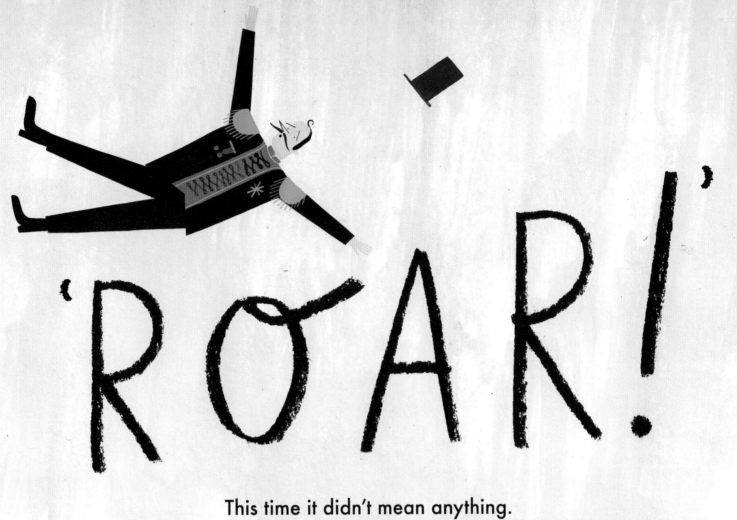

'ROAR!'

This time it didn't mean anything.
Sometimes a roar is just a roar.

The roar was so loud and so long and
so lonely that it blew the man
and his big hat far, far away.

Coralie heard Lion's roar echo
through the trees. 'I can't leave
my friend behind,' she thought.
She turned back to find him,

and there, walking away from the circus,
came acrobats and trumpeters, drummers
and jugglers, and best of all...

...Lion.

'ROAR!'

said Lion, which meant 'We're free at last!
Can we stay here with you?'

And Coralie hugged him, which meant, 'Of course.'

Now there's a group of friends
who live in the woods,
who don't like rules.

They swing through the trees,

and stand on their hands,

and juggle five squirrels at
a time – just for fun.

And every night, when the stars come out,
Coralie gives Lion a goodnight hug.
'I love you,' she says.
And Lion says...

'ROAR!'

Which means, 'I love you, too.'